Messy Mandy

PRESENTS

LUNCHTIME CHRONICLES

PEYTON BANKS

Copyright © 2023 by Peyton Banks

Editor: Emmy Ellis with Studioenp

Cover Design by Dar Albert of Wicked Smart Designs

This is a work of fiction. Names, characters, organizations, businesses, events, and incidents are a figment of the author's imagination and are used fictitiously. Any similarities to real people, businesses, locations, history, and events are a coincidence.

All rights reserved.

No part of this publication may be reproduced, distributed, or transmitted in any form or by any means, including photocopying, recording, or other electronic or mechanical methods, without the prior written permission of the publisher.

Information about the copyright permissions of the stock photos used can be provided upon request.

 Created with Vellum

blurb

He's so tasty, she just can't resist.

Niko Rusek had never been one to have female friends. Kizzie McCall blew into his life, and nothing was ever the same again.

But now she'd moved away and he realized she had filled a void in his life no one had ever claimed before. There was one thing he hadn't shared with Kizzie before she left and that was how much he needed and loved her.

Niko hadn't wanted to risk losing Kizzie by crossing the line, so he remained in the friend zone.

Kizzie McCall recently relocated home to help with the thriving family barbeque business. In doing so, she now lived across the country from her closest friend in the world.

Who was going to listen to her complain about her lousy dating adventures? Or give her advice when it came to the opposite sex?

She missed him like crazy.

Missed the way his eyes crinkled in the corners when he smiled, the sound of his laugh, his perfectly sculpted body...But Nico hadn't looked at her as anything other than a friend. Kizzie knew she wanted more and with Nico coming to visit her, she would take a chance.

The friend zone doesn't have to be forever? Or does it?

one

"Oh my God," Kizzie McCall groaned. She closed her eyes and basked in the taste exploding on her tongue. She was in heaven and didn't ever want to leave. She clutched the table with her free hand and wanted more. Kizzie lifted the muffin back to her mouth for another bite.

Pure ecstasy.

"If I didn't know any better, I'd say you were about to orgasm." Mykeisha chuckled.

Kizzie opened her eyes and met her cousin's twinkling brown ones. Food orgasms had to be a real thing, and if so, this muffin was getting her close.

Mykeisha raised her cup and took a sip of her coffee. "Should I be worried?"

"Only about my hips. I may be going back for another one." Kizzie giggled. She wiped her hands on her napkin and reached for her drink. She might purchase another one and take it with her on her way to work.

Kizzie and Mykeisha were as close as cousins could be. They had been raised together, seeing that their fathers were brothers. Both women shared warm brown skin, big almond-shaped brown eyes, and were about the same build. Many had mistaken them for sisters. The McCall genes were strong. Their fathers were three years apart and were always assumed to be twins.

"You have nothing to worry about with the way you work out. I'm sure your exercise regime will cancel out the calories from your breakfast," Mykeisha said, motioning to Kizzie's food. "Me, on the other hand, I think I gained two pounds just stepping foot in here."

"You chose the place." Kizzie grinned.

A few times a week, the girls met for breakfast before going off to work.

Baking 21-6 was the name of the popular bakery

they frequented quite often. It was open six days a week and for twenty-one hours a day, providing great teas and coffees, giving any popular coffee chain a run for their money. It was locally owned which made it even better, and many of the locals appreciated the late hours and being able to stop by either after work or before. No matter what time a customer stopped by, they could always count on the bakery to have fresh snacks available.

"Did you see Steve and Zoe are breaking up?" Mykeisha asked.

"Who?" Kizzie frowned, confused. She pondered hard on who her cousin could be talking about. She couldn't recall either of them having friends by that name.

"The actors." Mykeisha rolled her eyes. She pulled up her cell phone and turned it around to show a photo of the famous couple.

They were both high-paid actors who had been in major blockbuster movies. Kizzie shook her head and reached for her coffee again. Of course her cousin would be up to date with the latest celebrity gossip.

"Mandy said that he got caught cheating and Zoe is kicking him to the curb."

"You still reading that gossip column?" Kizzie inquired.

Her cousin was a diehard fan of the gossip columnist, Messy Mandy. The Lunchtime Dish had Mykeisha in a chokehold. She loved reading about all of the juicy details of the people who were featured. Mykeisha always spoke of Messy Mandy as if she knew the woman in real life. Secretly, Kizzie read the gossip as well, but only when she was bored.

At least that was what she told herself.

"Yes, I am!" Mykeisha gasped. Her hand flew to her chest as she stared at Kizzie in shock. "You speak as if you don't know me."

Kizzie tutted at her cousin's dramatics. There was no one on this planet who knew Mykeisha better than she did. They both knew things about the other that they would be taking to their graves.

"I'm not going to comment on that."

"Well, anyway, as I was saying. Obviously, Steve doesn't know how to keep his dick in his pants. He got caught in Vegas with three hookers, and it was said that he had got together with his costar, Kenya Knight." Mykeisha sat back. Her face was lit up as if she was sharing the juiciest of gossip.

"Who cares. They are celebrities. How does their love life affect ours when we don't have one?"

Ouch.

That even hurt to say it aloud. It was the truth, though. Both Mykeisha and Kizzie had horrible luck when it came to love. Mykeisha had been single for a while now, having given up on dating, while Kizzie had a not-so-impressive track record of bad dates and boyfriends.

Kizzie just didn't understand how either of them were single. They were both good catches. Mykeisha was the owner of a great bar and grille. She was beautiful, had brains, her own place, car, and money. Kizzie had recently relocated home to help out at their family's barbecue business. She was college educated, had a fabulous job, savings, and now got to work for her family.

She sighed, thinking of the big move. Relocating from San Francisco to Cleveland had been rough. She had lived in California ever since she had gone there for her undergraduate studies. Kizzie had received a full ride to Stanford University and obtained a business degree.

During her years there, she had fallen in love with the San Francisco area, which made her decision to stay easy. Kizzie loved history and art and loved strolling around parts of town to admire the Victorian homes, especially the famous painted ladies. The city fulfilled her love of art with the countless museums that were around, street fairs, and the food. Any type of food one could imagine; the city had amazing restaurants and cafés to visit. There was just something about the city that called to her.

But it wasn't just the city she missed.

She missed him.

Nikoderm Rusek, or better known as Niko, was why she felt homesick even though she had returned to the city where she'd grown up.

Niko was her best friend.

She missed his smile, his laugh, the way his eyes crinkled in the corners when he smiled. Niko could be a little gruff, and it had taken a while for her to get used to his quiet nature. He was a man of few words, but that was okay. She usually spoke enough for the both of them. They were complete opposites in every way. She'd grown up in a middle-class family surrounded by love while he'd grown up in a broken home with his brother.

They couldn't be more different, but somehow, their friendship worked.

"Well, who pissed in your Cheerios?" Mykeisha asked.

"What?" Kizzie blinked. She popped the last of the oversized muffin in her mouth and savored the final bite. "I don't know what you are talking about. Mandy doesn't know everything, and how are you reading her column? I thought she was going on vacation."

Kizzie froze. Mykeisha's eyes widened, and her smile grew wide.

Busted.

Kizzie was a fan of the column and had never let Mykeisha in on her little secret. She loved reading everything Messy Mandy had to spill.

"You whore. You are an undercover Lunchtime Dish reader!" Mykeisha balled up her napkin and threw it at Kizzie. "All this time you read her, too, and you never let on."

"I mean, you talk about the column all the time. How could I not check it out?" Kizzie laughed. She bent down and scooped up the napkin from the floor and placed it on the table between them. It was a guilty pleasure that she loved to indulge in. There were many nights she was home alone and found herself looking up the column online. With a glass of wine, it was good entertainment. "It's not like I'm dating anymore."

"What? But I thought you were on that new app. What's it called?" Mykeisha snapped her fingers.

"N2U online dating," Kizzie grumbled. She had thought she would have luck with online dating since she could screen men before she even spoke with them. But all the crazies still made it through. She had spent many nights complaining to Niko about her dates. He'd listen as he always did, then offered the same advice each time.

Block him.

"And it didn't work out?"

"Nope, and that's why I will be forever single." Kizzie sighed.

But would she? She had always hoped she would have found the special someone by now. She wasn't getting any younger. Her biological clock was ticking very loudly. At the age of thirty-two, she would have hoped to be at least in a committed relationship. The longest relationship she'd ever had with a member of the opposite sex was Niko.

And there were no benefits.

"What are you doing this weekend?"

Kizzie tried to hold back her smile, but she failed horribly. She had been waiting for this weekend for a while. Niko was coming to town to visit her. It would be the first time they'd seen each other since her move.

"Niko is coming to visit." She exhaled. Kizzie glanced down at her hands and tried to avoid Mykeisha's all-knowing gaze.

"Oh, so your man is coming to town." Mykeisha laughed.

"He's not my man." Kizzie reached up and tucked her thick dark hair behind her ear. She glanced up and found Mykeisha eyes filled with her usual deviousness. Her cousin always teased Kizzie about Niko. They were close friends and nothing more.

"I don't know why you keep lying to yourself. How do you handle him dating and sleeping with other women?"

"What? He can do whatever he wants. We are just friends," Kizzie said. Her voice sounded hollow even to her ears.

"Have you ever thought that the reason you can't find the perfect man for you is because you've already found him?" Mykeisha asked softly.

Kizzie inhaled sharply at how deep the conversation had turned. She blinked and looked away from her cousin and took in the busy bakery. There were plenty of people enjoying their morning coffee and breakfast. Had she realized that Niko was the man for her?

Yeah, she had. A while ago. She had been in love with him almost from the moment they had first met.

Sadly, Niko only saw her as his friend. He had never made a move on her or crossed any lines. The friend zone had been reserved for her, and she thought she would be happy there, but Mykeisha was right. Watching him with other women was torturous, and knowing that he was sleeping with them ate at her.

She'd failed at finding the right man for her because he was already in her life. It was a hard pill to swallow, but she hoped to change all of that this weekend. Kizzie didn't care if he was seeing someone. She couldn't remember the last chick he'd spoken about.

Her bestie was sort of a man whore.

He was always with some female who she didn't try to remember their name. None of the women were good enough for him. They couldn't give him what he needed.

Kizzie could.

She was going to tell him how she really felt

about him. Niko needed to know, and she had to get it off her chest. She didn't want to go another year with harboring this secret. It was festering inside her and was ready to be shared.

For far too long she had held these feelings for him inside. No more. She was going to claim her man.

"You and your imagination," Kizzie muttered. She didn't want to tell her cousin that she was going to put all of her cards on the table. For one, Mykeisha would never let her live it down. She had been saying for a while that Kizzie needed to stop playing around and go after Niko.

And two, Kizzie didn't want to admit it, but if Niko rejected her, she wanted to be able to lick her wounds in private. Not that Mykeisha wouldn't be there for her, but some things a woman had to deal with alone.

"Imagination? Girl, please. The entire world can see that the two of you are meant for each other. You just have blinders on and can't see." Mykeisha finished off her coffee and set her empty cup down on the table. "A man as fine as that will eventually get claws dug in him by some bitch."

"Mykeisha!" Kizzie laughed.

"One of them hoochies he's messing with will

eventually snag your man. Will you be able to deal with that? Attending Niko's wedding and you are not the bride?"

Her cousin had made a valid point.

There was no way in hell Kizzie would be able to be a guest at his wedding to some other woman.

Oh, hell no.

"Don't you burn that chicken like you did last time," Kizzie called out. She slammed the door to her car and headed toward the restaurant.

It was a beautiful warm day in Cleveland. It wasn't even noon yet, and the heat was already making its presence known. McCall's Barbecue was a well-known staple in the city. Their new restaurant was located in midtown and received plenty of traffic from the local business employees and the residents.

Kizzie's father, Charles, and his two brothers, Jeff and Donnie, had started McCall's Barbecue when they were in their mid-twenties. The men had a way around a grill and smoker. Their tasty barbecue had won awards at fairs around the country, and they were encouraged to share their talents with the community. The men had worked full time at a local factory and banded together to pool their savings.

In a short time, McCall's Barbecue was born.

The original building the restaurant was started in had been nicknamed 'the shack.' It had been a small white trailer that didn't allow for patrons to sit and enjoy their meal. It only allowed for a carry-out window, a tiny kitchen with a few grills out in the back. Kizzie remembered hanging out at the shack when she was a child. There hadn't been much room for children in the building so she, her brother, and cousins had spent much time out in the back with the grills. As time had moved on, the children of the McCall brothers began helping out at the restaurant wherever they were needed.

It was why Kizzie had such a love for her family's business. Their restaurant had grown in notoriety and was known as the best barbecue place in Northeast Ohio. Ten years ago, the McCalls purchased land and built a much larger restaurant that allowed for dining in. Business was booming, and Kizzie was hoping to help expand the brand with her extensive business background.

Her uncle Jeff, Mykeisha's father, glanced over

his shoulder at her and winked. His dark-brown skin was covered with a fine sheen of sweat. He pulled a towel out of his back jean pocket and wiped his forehead before returning it. The scent wavering in the air was something that she had found herself homesick for when she was in California.

"Who burned chicken? Ain't no one burning chicken around here." He barked a laugh.

She stopped near him and gave him a one-armed hug. He drew away from her, a twinkle in his eye. In that instant, she could see Mykeisha in her uncle's expression.

"Don't y'all young folk like meat blackened? Isn't that a thing?"

"There's a big difference between blackened and burnt, Uncle." She snickered.

Jeff opened a grill cover, and a billow of smoke wafted up to the sky. There was nothing like the scent of roasting meat. Even though she had recently eaten breakfast, she felt a little pang of hunger. She would never tire of the delectable meats, the sweet and smokey sauce her family had patented, and the family secret side dishes they sold.

"It still sold, didn't it?" he asked while flipping over the ribs.

"No, Uncle Donnie refused to offer it to the public. He didn't want our good name ruined," she replied.

"What?" He spun around and eyed her.

That was her cue to leave. If he wanted to argue his brother down about selling burnt meat then that would be between them.

"All it would need was extra sauce," he said.

"Talk to Donnie about it." She blew him a kiss and headed inside.

Her uncle just didn't want to admit he had burned that chicken. Kizzie went into the break room that was in the back of the building. The room was empty. The only sound was the television mounted on the wall.

Kizzie beelined over to her locker. She put her purse up and took out her clean apron and put it on. It was Friday, and the lunch rush was always crazy, which would be perfect.

It would keep her from thinking too much about Niko coming to town. She hadn't spoken to him in a couple of days. She didn't have any worries that he wasn't going to come. If he had changed his mind or something had come up, he would have called her. Niko was always a man to keep his word.

The butterflies in her stomach fluttered.

It would be good to see her friend again. It had been way too long since she had felt his arms wrap around her in a hug. She missed being able to breathe in his scent in those few seconds she was in his embrace.

She closed her locker and left the break room. Walking into the kitchen, she was accosted by the aromas of the different foods being cooked. Her father and Uncle Donnie were hard at work.

"Hey, Daddy." She moved over to him and stood on her tiptoes and kissed him on the cheek.

Charles McCall, Sr., was a man who lit up the room with his smile. If anyone were to describe the perfect father, a picture of him would be included. This man loved her and her brother unconditionally. There wasn't anything he wouldn't do for his children.

Charles had always been a part of her life. He and her mother had flown out to California just to visit her when she was in college because they'd missed her. They'd stocked up her apartment with food and ensured she had money in her bank account. They would go out and explore San Francisco together. Charles hadn't wanted his little girl wanting for anything while she'd been away from him. When she and her brother, Junior, were growing up, their father had been there for every recital, sporting event, and parent meeting. He didn't miss any part of their childhood.

"It's about time you rocked up, pumpkin. I thought you were going be a no-show." Charles grinned.

"And miss seeing your handsome face?" She laughed.

Her father wrapped her up in his arms and squeezed her tight. She returned the embrace. Kizzie was never too old to receive a hug from her father.

"Oh, please. This old ugly mug?" He released her and turned back to the counter where he was preparing his famous macaroni and cheese. He was a stickler when it came to his cheese blend and believed that it should only be manually shredded and mixed himself.

"Me and Mykeisha met for breakfast," she said. She leaned against the steel counter and folded her arms in front of her while she watched her father work. She had learned this recipe at his hip in the kitchen of the home she'd grown up in. By the time Kizzie was fifteen, she'd known her way around the kitchen.

"How's that niece of mine?" he asked.

"And why hasn't she been by here this week?" Donnie asked from his place in front of the industrial stove. He was stirring a pot that looked suspiciously like baked beans. Their family believed in making everything fresh, and baked beans was one thing the McCall brothers did not purchase in a can.

"She's doing well and has been very busy over at her bar," Kizzie replied smoothly.

The McCall brothers had never understood Mykeisha's need to run her own business. According to them, all of the McCall children should have some part of the McCall Barbecue empire. Even Donnie's children helped out when they could.

"Do you need help back here?" Kizzie glanced around and tried to figure out where she could start. It looked as if they had everything under control.

"For now we should be good," her father said. He glanced over at Donnie. "You need Kizzie for anything?"

"Not at the moment. I'll let you know," Donnie replied.

"I'll go out front and see if they need help. I'm sure the rush will be starting anytime soon." She gave a wave and headed to the front of the restaurant. If it wasn't busy, then she would go into the office and work on the books. Kizzie was utilizing her fancy degree she had earned at Stanford University. She was excited to help her family out this way. She had reviewed the finances of the business, and they were in talks of possibly opening a second location.

Their family employed a lot of young people who were down on their luck, needing a second chance in life. It was their way of contributing to the community. She waved to a few of the employees as she walked toward the counter. She arrived in the doorway that led to the front and paused.

It would appear she was right.

There was already a line forming, and it was almost to the door.

Patrons were already sitting at a few tables, and within an hour, Kizzie was sure the place would be packed.

"Hey, Sarah. I'll jump on the other register and start taking orders." Kizzie smiled at the young woman.

Sarah had just celebrated her year anniversary with the restaurant. She was a great asset and a hard worker. She was a kid who had aged out of the foster system and was trying to make it in life.

"Thank you." Relief filled Sarah's face. She reached up and brushed her thick auburn hair behind her ear. She turned back to the next customer. "Do you want your sauce on the wings or on the side?"

Kizzie moved over to the open register and waved for the next customer in line. She gave a wide smile and greeted the couple who came forward.

This was what she needed. A busy afternoon to keep her mind off of how she was going to seduce her best friend.

two

Niko Rusek guided his rental car through the light traffic of Cleveland. It had been a long flight from San Francisco, and his body was tired. He hated to be confined in one spot for long, and to be seated next to someone he didn't know made it even worse.

Niko wasn't the type of person who liked to be around other people. He had flown business class since he was on the tall side at six foot three, and with his lengthy legs he needed the extra room. There had been an older gentleman next to him who had tried to make conversation on the flight. Niko had immediately pulled out his headphones, threw his hoodie over his head, and closed his eyes.

He didn't do small conversations.

"What the fuck are you doing?" Niko growled, watching a vehicle in front of him cut over two lanes.

Car horns sounded as the idiot made their turn. It was a wonder that person hadn't caused an accident.

Niko ran a hand through his hair and guided his car to a stop. Another fucking light was causing a delay in his trip. He sat back and wished he was on his bike instead. He needed to feel the wind in his hair, the powerful machine between this thighs.

Riding his bike gave him the freedom he always wanted to feel. He'd be out for hours on the weekends, even some nights when he couldn't sleep. Niko had spent majority of his life around motorcycles. When he was younger, he'd had a fascination with them. His older brother, Will, had gotten a job at a bike shop, and Niko used every excuse he could think of to hang out there.

The owner, George, had been the closest thing to a saint in young Niko's eyes. Home life hadn't been the best. His old man had been a drunk, and his mother turned a blind eye to anything his father had done to him or his brother.

But George had seen something in the Rusek brothers. Maybe the old man knew that if he didn't hire the boys on, they would have ended up in the streets with the wrong crowd. If he hadn't, he would have been right. Ten years ago, George had decided it was time for him to retire. His body and hands wouldn't allow him to work the machinery the way it required.

Will and Niko had offered to buy the shop.

George had sold it to them without a second thought.

Will and Niko renovated the shop and gave it a new name—Precision Motors. They took what they had learned from the old man, and with their business sense, they elevated Precision Motors to a higher level. They had clientele a mile long, and their shop was one of the top motorcycles repair shops in all of California.

Niko was proud of what he and his brother had accomplished. They had come from nothing and had made it. Niko could always count on him. Will had left home at eighteen, and the minute Niko had turned seventeen, he'd left and joined him. They would rather have struggled together than to remain in that hellhole of a home they had grown up in. The last Niko heard of his parents was his father had died of a drug overdose and their mother was now on her fifth husband.

He blew out a deep breath and tried not to think of his upbringing. He had done well with himself and had all the money needed, owned a home, cars, and multiple bikes. The only thing missing was someone to share all of that with. He secretly wanted a family of his own. He'd never admitted it to anyone and had buried it deep down inside. He had been focused on building his business and enjoying all the spoils that came with being a successful businessman.

But then a short brown-skinned woman with the biggest personality had blown into his life, and nothing had ever been the same.

Kizzie McCall.

He had to admit, he had never truly befriended many people. The amount of people he would consider a true friend he could count on one hand.

But Kizzie, she was different.

Niko remembered the night he had met her like it had happened yesterday. He and Will had just secured the purchase of Precision Motors and had gone out for celebratory drinks. They hadn't even come up with a new name for their shop yet. But two young brothers in their twenties purchasing a thriving motorcycle repair shop called for a cele-bration.

They had gone out to the local watering hole they both enjoyed. Ten minutes inside, and Will had become distracted with a little blonde, leaving Niko at the bar alone.

"It sure is crowded tonight," Niko murmured. He leaned against the counter, his eyes locked on the television screen. The 49ers were on, and he had money on the game. They were up by fourteen, and he sent up a little prayer that they would keep the lead. One more quarter to go, and if they won, he was due to win a cool thousand dollars.

"No, you don't have to buy me a drink," a husky feminine voice announced.

Niko took a sip of his vodka that he had been nursing and ignored her. Something about her voice did pique his interest, but he wasn't here for women.

"But thank you anyway."

She gave a nervous laugh, and something about it made him curious to see what she looked like. He turned slightly and saw a beautiful woman with flawless brown skin, dark hair pulled up into a ponytail. She was much shorter than the jerk standing next to her. The guy was invading her personal space, and from her expression, she didn't appreciate it.

"It's only a drink, baby," the guy sneered. He raised his arm for the bartender who was busy preparing a

mixed concoction. "A pretty little thing like yourself must be thirsty."

"Again, thank you for the offer, but I don't want another drink, I have one." She raised the glass in her hand.

Her eyes cut over to Niko, and instantly, he felt as if he had been punched in the gut. His breath lodged in his throat as he took in the silent plea in her eyes.

Niko turned away for a moment. It was none of his business what went on. The bar had security and a few bouncers he was cool with. He glanced over by the door. Butch, who had been manning it, appeared to be handling something outside. Niko's gaze roamed around the bar, and he didn't see the others. He released a curse under his breath.

"Do women even know what they want? Whatcha drinkin'?" the jerk face asked. He sidled closer to the woman who stepped away but bumped into another man behind her.

She was practically trapped.

"Shit," Niko muttered. He knocked back the rest of his drink and held off a wince as the clear liquid burned its way down his throat. He reached for the bottle he had ordered when he and Will had arrived. He poured himself another drink. If he was going to do something *as crazy as get rid of a creep for a woman, he might as well enjoy his nice expensive vodka first.*

"You know what? I'm going to leave," she said.

"Nah, baby. You don't have to go," Asshole said.

"Get your hand off me," the woman snapped.

That did it for Niko. His gaze slid to her, and he took in the guy holding her arm in a firm grip. Niko moved behind him, resting his hand on the jerk's shoulder. It had been a long while since he'd gotten into a bar fight. He'd admit he and his brother had been in a few in their younger years. Now that he was a businessman, he didn't think that would look good, but he wasn't going to stand for a man not adhering to a woman's wishes.

"The woman wants to be left alone, buddy," Niko growled. His chest burned from the warmth of the alcohol.

"Nobody asked you." The guy swung around and shrugged off Niko's hold. He faced Niko but still had the woman's arm in his grasp.

She cried out and stumbled with him as he moved toward Niko.

"Didn't have to. The woman obviously didn't want to hurt your feelings, but I don't give a shit about them. Get the fuck out of here and leave her alone," Niko snarled.

He inched closer to the idiot, standing toe to toe with him. Niko quickly sized him up. The asshole had a little more weight on him around the abdomen area. His eyes were dilated, a sign he probably had something in his system.

"Now let her go."

A small crowd now gathered around them. Niko hoped one of the bouncers would be over so he wouldn't have to beat this guy to a pulp.

"Why? You want her for yourself? Go find you own piece of puss—"

Niko didn't give him a chance to finish his sentence. His fist shot out and landed a hard punch to the side of the guy's face. Pain exploded throughout Niko's knuckles, but he ignored it. The guy staggered back, releasing the young lady. The crowd roared, the onlookers appearing unfazed. Instead of dispersing, they remained where they were as if hungry for a fight.

"What's going on here?" Butch hollered, barreling through the crowd.

Behind him was Rich, another bouncer.

"You son of a bitch!" the guy yelled.

He dashed forward, but Butch caught him up in a bear hug. The guy was no match for Butch's strength. The bouncer was a former NFL player and had fought in an amateur MMA league.

"*Now don't go doing something you'll regret,*" Butch warned.

"*What happened?*" Rich asked, coming over to stand by Niko. Rich was a cop who was moonlighting as a bouncer to make ends meet.

"*The asshole wouldn't leave her alone.*" Niko motioned to his right, but he didn't see the woman. She had disappeared through the melee. He ran a hand through his hair and shook his head. Where did she go? Niko quickly gave a recount of what had happened.

Butch dragged the unruly guy away through the thinning crowd. Apparently, since there wasn't going to be an all-out brawl, they were no longer interested.

"*Well, thanks for stepping in. It's crazy tonight.*" Rich slapped him on the shoulder.

Niko gave him a small salute and turned back to the counter where his bottle and glass sat. He reached for the glass and pulled it toward him. A presence arrived at his side. He glanced over and found the small woman standing with an ice pack in her hand.

"*Here. This is for you,*" she said softly. She closed the gap between them and took his hand in hers. "*You didn't have to do that.*"

"*He had it coming,*" Niko said.

He didn't know why, but he allowed her to take his hand and rest the ice on it. Her soft hand was gentle as *she held the cold bag to his knuckles. Her big brown eyes flicked up to his. His breath was taken away by how gorgeous she was. Niko wasn't one to be stunned by women, but there was something about her.*

"He did. He was close to getting kicked in the balls." She smiled. She hopped up on the stool next to him, elevating her to his height. "Kizzie."

"Huh?"

"My name is Kizzie. Kizzie McCall. I might as well introduce myself to the person who saved me." She giggled.

Kizzie tenderly held the ice on his hand while shifting to face him. She stared at him for a moment before he realized she was waiting on him.

"Niko." He cleared his throat. He glanced around the bar and didn't see anyone who appeared to be waiting on Kizzie. He turned his attention back to her. "Why are you here alone?"

Kizzie's eyes lowered in what he assumed was embarrassment. She shrugged and blew out a deep breath.

"I was stood up. I had met this guy online, and we were supposed to meet here, but he didn't show."

What kind of man would stand up a woman like Kizzie? She was beautiful, and Niko could tell she had a heart of gold. He had never had anyone, much less a stranger, try to take care of him. She could have easily just left during the altercation, but instead she'd gone and got an icepack for his hand.

"Whoever the fucker is don't deserve you." Niko reached over with his free hand and removed the ice pack. He'd had worse injuries before, and this was nothing. "Thank you."

"It's the least I can do." She glanced down at her watch, a smile playing on her lips. She hopped down from the stool and snagged her small purse from the counter. "It's getting late. I better go. I should have never agreed to meet him. I had a feeling he wouldn't show."

"I'll walk you to your car," Niko said.

He didn't know what had gotten into him. A strange sense came over him at the thought of her walking to her car at this time of night. There was no telling who was lingering out in the parking lot. Niko tossed a few bills on the counter. He didn't know where his brother had disappeared to. He'd cuss him out in the morning for abandoning him when they were supposed to be celebrating.

"You don't have to. I'll be fine."

"Nonsense. I'm leaving now anyway." He cupped her elbow and guided her through the crowd and out the door.

That night, his life changed forever.

Niko's stomach growled at the aroma of meat smoking floating through the air. He stalked toward the door of McCall's Barbecue. The restaurant's parking lot was packed with cars. If the food was as good as it smelled, he could see why there were no parking spots available.

He pulled open the door, and the scent of food accosted him even harder than it had outside. He inhaled, and his stomach gave another warning growl. He hadn't bothered to eat before he'd caught his flight, nor had he eaten on the plane. His stomach was now reminding him that he needed sustenance.

The decor of the restaurant was simple and casual. Upbeat R&B music flowed through the speakers, colorful artwork was showcased along the wall, and there was plenty of laughter going around, giving the place a down-home feel. It gave Niko the same feeling he had experienced when Kizzie had taken him to her sorority sister's cookout. He'd had a good time that day, and the few minutes of being in her family's restaurant reminded him of it.

The line that went to the door was moving fast.

Two women stood at the registers, taking the customers' orders. Niko's gaze zeroed in on the woman with her perfect brown skin, Coke-bottle-frame figure dressed in jeans and a shirt.

It had been six months since he had seen Kizzie in person, and she still took is breath away. Her warm smile always relaxed him and melted away any stressors. At the moment her attention was on an elderly couple who were placing their order.

"Will you be dining in with us? Or taking your food home to go?" Kizzie asked.

She always had a way with people. There was something about her that drew everyone to her. Even the likes of him. He wasn't the easiest person to get along with, but for Kizzie, it was like a walk in the park.

Today her dark hair was pulled up into a pony-tail with a few wayward wisps hanging around her face. She had little bags underneath her eyes, but her smile was still bright. Kizzie always put everyone before herself. She was tired and probably wasn't taking good care of herself. Niko didn't have to ask how much she was working. He was sure she was putting in long hours. It was an honorable thing for her to leave the city she had grown to love, her job, and friends to move back home to help her family.

She hadn't noticed him yet. It was no secret that he was coming to visit. Niko had the opportunity to take an earlier flight. He would have to admit that he was anxious to see Kizzie. They spoke on the phone regularly, and she had even convinced him to use the video call option on their phones.

But nothing was the same as having her near him, forcing her hugs on him or having the scent of her perfume on his clothes or in his home. He truly did miss having her around. That was why he had traveled across the country.

Niko had come to the realization that he was in love with Kizzie McCall. He hadn't realized it until after she had gone, but it had explained so much. He, who was never lonely on the weekends, had begun to find that all of the women he approached were lacking. None of them appealed to him. Niko tried to remember the last woman he'd had sex with but couldn't even bring the image of her face to mind, much less recall her name.

He hadn't known the problem. Instead, he'd thrown himself into his work. He'd soon found himself at the shop seven days a week. They were closed on Sundays, but Niko still went in, citing that he was trying to ensure all projects were up to date.

He hadn't shared this information with Kizzie. Instead, he'd listened to all her dating horror stories. He'd found himself growing angry with each new story without knowing why.

Was it a newfound jealousy? Was it because he wanted to be the one taking Kizzie out on a date? To be the one kissing her soft lips? Hearing about other men, where they had taken her and how they kissed her had Niko seeing red. They both drew the line at sex stories.

Well, Kizzie had established that rule years ago after she'd learned of the amount of women he went through. One morning, she had let herself into his condo as two women he had partied with were preparing to leave. It was the last time she had let herself into his home unannounced. Niko winced, remembering their state of undress when they'd stumbled upon Kizzie in the kitchen making coffee.

Niko would never apologize for having a healthy sexual appetite and the drive to have fun. There was no harm in fun if both parties were adults and had the same goal in mind. But something had changed inside him. He hadn't liked the hurt expression in her eyes. After that, he'd shielded her away from the women he slept with.

Niko finally arrived at the front of the line. Kizzie had yet to recognize him. The other cashier waved to him, but he shook his head. He nodded to Kizzie and put his finger to his lips. He sent the server a wink, eliciting a shy smile from the young girl.

"Can I help you?" Kizzie asked. Her gaze finally landed on him. She froze in place before her lips broke into a wide grin. She took a step back from the counter, racing around toward him. "Niko!"

He barked a hefty laugh as her smaller frame slammed into him. He automatically wrapped her up into a tight hug. It had been six long months since he had held her in his arms. Kizzie's arms slid around him and squeezed as if her life depended on it.

"I can't believe you're here," she murmured. She leaned her head back, meeting his gaze.

The memory of her beauty didn't do the real thing justice. If Niko didn't know better, he would say she had grown even more beautiful.

"What are you talking about? You knew I was coming," he replied. Niko ignored the curious stares of the customers in line behind them. He had flown across the country to see her and didn't care if they grew disgruntled. He dared someone to say something to him. They wouldn't like his response.

"You weren't supposed to arrive until later. How did you sneak into town?" Kizzie asked. She wore a wide grin while her arms tightened around him.

Niko was captivated by her smile. There wasn't anything he wouldn't do for her at that moment.

"There was an earlier flight available, so I took that one," he admitted.

Kizzie glanced around him at the people in line, then looked over at the young lady who was taking a customer's order.

"Sarah, would you be okay if I left a little early?" Kizzie asked. She pulled away from Niko but entwined their fingers together.

Holding Kizzie's hand came as naturally as breathing. She was always a touchy-feely person, and it was something Niko had to get used to.

"You can go. I can handle this line, and if I can't, I'll call for Dwayne to come help me," Sarah said. A sly smile appeared on her face. "Have fun, and I'll see you later."

"I need to go home and shower before we go anywhere. I'm smelling like barbecue." Kizzie spun back to him. She had a flushed look on her face, and her eyes were bright with excitement.

This was what he'd missed. Even when he had a shitty day, he could count on Kizzie's energy to lift his spirits.

Niko pulled her to him and bent his head down to nuzzle the crook of her neck. He inhaled and took in the scent of smoke and hickory along with the faint hint of her floral perfume. She stiffened slightly before leaning into him.

"Smells good to me," he murmured. He lifted his head and met her gaze. He'd never been so bold before to cross a line like this, but he didn't care. He'd come to Cleveland for one reason.

To claim his woman.

three

"What is smelling so good?" Niko asked.

He followed behind her as they entered her home. Kizzie's thoughts were currently scrambled. She couldn't stop thinking about Niko sniffing her neck. For the entire drive, she'd kept replaying it over and over in her mind. If he hadn't been holding her up, she would have melted to the floor in a puddle.

"I took the liberty of grabbing us something to eat before we left." Kizzie shut the door and locked it. She leaned back against it, holding the bag with the to-go containers she had packed.

Get it together, girl.

She didn't know what the move had meant, but

she welcomed it. While in the car, Niko had filled her in on the happenings at the shop, his brother, and a few things he had remodeled around his house. It was funny to her that the things she had told him needed to be updated, he'd waited until she had left to actually do them.

Didn't he know she knew what he needed more than he did?

"I'm glad you did. I'm starving," Niko said. He continued on, exploring her small home.

She smirked watching him stroll through her living room. He paused near her bookshelves where a few picture frames were displayed. Niko picked up one of them and stared at it. Kizzie knew which one it was without moving from her spot.

It was a picture from his thirty-fifth birthday party she had thrown for him. Niko had protested her organizing a party in his honor. Of course, him not wanting a party meant she had to do it. He tried to hide behind his tough-guy façade, but she saw right through it. Earlier that year, his brother, Will, had shared with her that with their upbringing, they had never had birthday parties. Kizzie had been shocked at the news. She, who'd had a wonderful childhood, had birthdays that were memorable because of the parties. It wasn't even just the shindigs but how special she felt having a day focused on her. Friends and family would come to hang out, and they always had a blast.

Kizzie had wanted to give Niko that feeling.

Four years ago, she had thrown him one hell of a party. It was a night she would never forget. She had rented out a bar for the evening, hired a DJ, a few dancers, and with Will's help, invited a bunch of people who knew him and Niko.

They'd all showed up.

The night had been wild and fun. Good food, entertainment, and drinks were all they needed. She had never seen Niko smile so much. He had even blown out candles on his cake. It was then her thoughts about him had started to morph into more.

The photographer she had hired had snapped a picture of the two of them. Both of them had been well into their cups, but it was the look of pure happiness on Niko's face that made this one of her favorite photos of them.

"I was so fucking drunk that night." Niko chuckled.

"If I remember right, we all were." She laughed. Pushing off the door, she went into the kitchen. Her home was a cute rental that was the perfect size for her. She hadn't wanted to purchase immediately when she'd moved back to Cleveland. Her house in San Francisco had sold fast for well over what she had paid for it.

Her current living space was an open floor plan and had soft neutral colors. The kitchen was a little cozy. There wasn't much room for two people to prepare meals. It hadn't been a problem since it was just her, but now, seeing Niko walk around in the house, she realized how small the place truly was. Niko was a large man and took up a lot of space.

"I grabbed a few things." She set the bag on the counter and quickly washed her hands. She arranged the containers and began opening them. The aroma of sweet hickory filled the air. Even though she was around the barbecue pits and food all day, she never tired of it. Her father's and uncles' cooking was just that good.

She took a couple of plates out of the cabinet. Looking at all the food she'd packed, she came to the realization that she may have grabbed too much. She hadn't been too sure what Niko had a taste for but she couldn't go wrong with the chicken wings smothered in sauce, or the ribs, fries, and standard sides of greens, mac and cheese, and baked beans. She reached for one of her favorite items that her family had won several awards for.

The polish boy.

It was a Cleveland barbecue staple that everyone needed in their life. A nice, thick juicy kielbasa sausage nestled in a soft warm bun, a layer of fries covered with barbecue sauce, and a pile of coleslaw to top it off.

Kizzie's mouth watered at the thought of eating one.

"Whatever you put on my plate, I will eat," Niko announced from the doorway. His bright-blue eyes were riveted on her. He combed his fingers through his dark hair, pushing it back away from his face.

Kizzie wasn't sure if he knew it or not, but that move was so damn sexy. She squeezed her thighs tight, sensing her core pulse with need. He folded his arms in front of him. His arms, covered in tattoos, were on display. She had never been an arm woman, but at the moment, she had a hard time tearing her eyes away from his.

"That's what I'm counting on," she said, turning away. She picked up the two foil-covered polish boys and set them on the plates. Her breath caught in her throat as Niko pushed off the doorway and sauntered into the kitchen.

Where was he going? Kizzie exhaled slowly, trying to will her racing heart to calm down. Niko moved behind her and trapped her against the counter by placing his hands on it, either side of her.

Kizzie froze in place. Her heart ignored her plea and sped up ever faster. At this rate, it was going to pound its way out of her chest.

It took great concentration to make her hands move. She began working the foil and opened the first polish boy.

"What in God's name is that?" Niko murmured.

His hard frame was against her. Kizzie's eyes fluttered shut for a moment. She basked in the feeling of him. She bit her lip and opened her eyes. She had imagined feeling him pressed close to her, and now it was a reality. Her thoughts raced.

Did he have feelings for her that were not the friendly kind? He shifted slightly, leaning over to look over her shoulder, and she took notice of something pushing at her ass.

A large jean-covered bulge was resting on her bottom.

Good Lord above.

She had to bite back a whimper and keep herself from rubbing on his cock.

"It's a...um..." Her thoughts were escaping her,

and she just couldn't get her brain to formulate any words that made sense. The scent of Niko and the feel of him had her body going haywire.

Here it was, she had plans to seduce him, and here he was, wrecking her plans with one simple move. Kizzie stood up straight, the move causing her ass to rub on him.

"It's a polish boy," she said, finally able to get her thoughts together.

"A what?" He laughed. He moved the foil out of the way to reveal more of the sandwich. The aroma of the sauce and meat greeted them. "I may not know much about my roots, but I can tell you, that is not Polish."

"You're Polish?" Her voice ended on a squeak.

She glanced over her shoulder at him, his blue eyes meeting hers. This was news to her. For as long as she had known him, he hadn't talked much about his family. His parents had been horrible and his childhood filled with abuse and neglect. It wasn't often he spoke of his parents. His father was dead and his mother was still alive, but that was pretty much all she knew.

"How did you not know that? My given name is Nikoderm Rusek. Polish descendants." He shrugged as if this would be common knowledge.

"How the hell am I supposed to know your nationality just by a name?" She raised an eyebrow at him. Seriously, how would she know that? Did he know her family's nationality from the name Kizzie McCall? Many people thought her name, Kizzie, was short for something, but it wasn't. Her mother had just loved the name and had given it to her.

"Well, now you do. My great-grandparents emigrated to the States around the nineteen thirties." He jerked his chin toward the plate. "And I can definitely tell you no one in my family ever served anything that looked like that."

Kizzie chortled and turned back around and picked up the dog. She spun around and held it up to his lips.

"Well, Polish boy, have your first taste of a Cleveland polish boy." She giggled.

His eyes narrowed on her for a moment before his lips curved up in the corner. His tough-guy persona didn't work on her. It may have everyone else convinced, but not her. He leaned down and opened his mouth. She guided the dog to him, helping him get his first bite of the sandwich. As she expected, it was messy. Barbecue sauce and a smear of the coleslaw rested on the edges of his mouth and chin.

They laughed as the sandwich practically fell apart in her hand. Thankfully, with the foil coverings, none of it landed on the floor. It was common for this to happen. A messy sandwich was the best kind to have.

Niko, covered with barbecue and coleslaw sauce on his mouth, was one of the sexiest things she had ever seen.

He chewed a few times before finally swallowing.

"That has to be one of the best things I have eaten in a long while." Niko shook his head while his gaze dropped down to her hands.

He had yet to remove his hands from the counter, leaving her to feed him, which she didn't mind. She raised the dog again, and he took another bite. More of the sauce landed on his lips and chin.

Her attention zeroed in on his lips, watching him chew. Once he swallowed, she reached up and wiped the corner of his mouth with her finger. She held her breath and moved her finger to his lips that parted. His tongue snuck out and licked the barbecue sauce off her skin.

Kizzie inhaled sharply, suddenly needing to finish what she'd stared. She wiped the other side of his mouth and again offered her finger for him.

His eyes met with hers as he again cleaned her finger.

"I'm glad you like it," she said. Her voice sounded husky to her. She glanced down at her other hand that held what was left of the sandwich.

"I do, but I don't want to eat all of it. Here, allow me."

Niko took the foil from her and stepped toward her, pushing her up against the counter. He held the kielbasa to her mouth. Kizzie opened it wide so she could take a bite. The hunger pains she had felt when she'd first left work were no longer there.

The hunger she experienced now was not for food.

The taste of the kielbasa's spiciness, the hickory of the barbecue sauce, and the sweetness of the coleslaw exploded on her tongue. This was the type of meal one savored, but she had other things on her mind right now. She finished chewing and swallowed hard.

This was what she had wanted for so long, and finally, she was going to get what she wanted.

"You have a little bit here," Niko murmured.

His large hand came to her face, swiping the sauce off her lips with his finger. He slid it along her bottom lip, his gaze pinned on her mouth. She parted her lips and sucked his finger inside.

"Fuck."

Kizzie bit back a moan. She ensured there was no sauce left on his finger. She twirled her tongue around it, showcasing what she was capable of. Her breath caught in her throat at the thought of licking the length of something else of his.

Niko raised his eyes to meet hers. The desire burning in his bright-blue eyes fueled her on.

Niko wanted her.

Not as a friend.

But as a woman.

He tossed the remains of the sandwich on the counter and closed the gap between them. He lowered his head and slammed his mouth on hers. Kizzie's lips parted, granting his tongue entrance. He swept in like an angry storm rolling, intent on destruction. Her breath was snatched from her.

Kizzie had no chance to celebrate, but the joy that filled her was being overrun with the mounting desire that flooded her. Niko's kiss had her melting against him. Had he not been standing in front of her, she would have fallen to the floor. Her hands had been resting on his waist but immediately began moving on their own accord.

They eased underneath his t-shirt and met his warm skin. She gasped, wanting to see and feel more. She hooked her fingers on the edge of his shirt and tugged it up and over his head, breaking their kiss. Her gaze greedily took in his perfectly sculpted pectoral muscles and traveled down to the multiple ridges of his abdomen. His arms were covered with tattoos, but his chest and abdomen were free of them.

She tossed his shirt onto the floor and stepped forward, pressing a kiss to his hairless chest.

"Kizzie," Niko murmured.

"Hmm?" She continued her exploration of him. She snuck her tongue out and trailed it along his skin.

"Do you know what you're doing?" He reached out and gripped the back of her head with both of his hands and forced her to look up at him.

She gave a small smile and nodded.

"Something I've been wanting to do for years," she replied honestly.

"Is that so?" His fingers glided into her hair, and he tugged it free from the ponytail holder. Her dark tresses fell around her shoulders. He leaned and pressed a chaste kiss to her lips. "Then I would say we have been wanting the same."

Her heart leaped up. How had she not known that he was digging her? Could they have taken this step years ago? Would they have been ready?

"I've always said we think alike." She tittered.

She reached up and pulled his head down to her, offering her lips for him. He claimed them without hesitation. A few kisses from him were not enough. Now that she'd had a taste of Niko, she wanted to sample all of him.

Niko's big hands slipped her shirt off. Their lips returned to each other while they removed their clothing. There was an urgency between them that needed to be met.

Kizzie's bra floated to the floor. Niko lifted his head to take her in. She stood still while his gaze roamed her naked mounds. She bit her lip, his perusal continuing on down her body. Only her panties remained as well as his boxer briefs. She took advantage of the pause to take him in as well. She'd seen him in only shorts before, but not his underwear, so this time it was different.

He was currently supporting a large erection that tented his underwear.

"Oh my God," she whimpered. Her eyes were locked on his bulge.

Niko's finger tipped her chin upwards, forcing

her to tear her gaze away from his cock. She licked her lips, and a growl erupted from him.

"Patience, Kizzie," he murmured. Niko bent down and hefted her up by the backs of her knees and sat her on the edge of the counter, away from the forgotten food. He stepped inside the valley of her thighs and softly kissed her. "We've waited a long time for this. We need—"

"If you say slow, I'm going to punch you," she interjected. She didn't need slow and easy. At the moment, she ached to feel his cock fill her up and take her hard. She wanted all of him and didn't want to wait for anything.

"You've never had any patience."

"It ain't going to start today," she muttered.

She reached for him, wanting to pull his mouth toward hers, but he resisted.

"You don't get to run the show," he warned.

There was a glint in his eyes that had her core clenching. His gaze dropped to her breasts. His hands came up to cup them. Her mounds fit perfectly in his large hands. She bit her lip again as he rolled her nipples between his fingers. He dropped his head down and captured one of her nipples with his mouth. She moaned, throwing her head back. His tongue bathed her pebbled bud, teasing her.

Kizzie combed her fingers through his thick, soft hair. He took his time nipping, licking, and suckling her breast, dragging his tongue over to the other one. Kizzie's breaths were coming in pants. Her pussy was drenched. Wetness poured from her. Her core pulsed, needing his cock.

Niko lifted his head. His hand arrived at the back of her neck and guided her to him. He nipped at her lips, soothing them with his tongue. Her lips parted. allowing him to enter. He swept in like a raging storm, consuming her. Kizzie leaned forward, her legs pressing against him to hold him in place.

Niko tore his lips from hers and trailed hot kisses along her jawline and down toward her neck. Kizzie arched toward him, angling her neck away for him. Niko dragged his teeth over her skin. His hands slid down her torso and came to rest on her waist.

"Is your pussy wet for me, Kizzie?" Niko's lips brushed her neck.

She whimpered and nodded.

His hands tightened on her. "I can't hear you."

"Yes," she breathed.

His hands coasted down her thighs, parting them wider. She rested her hands on his shoulders, not wanting to take them off him. Niko moved her silky panties to the side.

"Why aren't these off?"

"You didn't take them off." She smirked.

"There you go with that smart mouth of yours."

His deep chuckle sent a tremor through her. His finger parted her slick folds and slipped between them, running the length of her pussy. Kizzie dug her nails into his skin, holding still. Her lungs burned from the lack of air. She held her breath and met his gaze.

Niko's smile disappeared. "Fuck."

He pushed a finger deep inside her. Kizzie cried out, no longer able to hold still. She arched her hips toward him. It had been too long since she'd been with someone intimately, and she wouldn't want it to be with anyone else but Niko.

He didn't say another word but lowered his head to her. He took her mouth in a bruising kiss. She wrapped her arms around his neck, returning the kiss with fervor. He withdrew his finger momentarily before thrusting two up. She stiffened and tore her mouth from his with a gasp.

"Niko," she ground out.

"You're fucking small," he muttered. He nestled his face into the crook of her neck, continually pumping her core with his fingers. He rotated them, widening the girth of them. He drove them harder and faster within her.

Kizzie's body trembled uncontrollably. The sensations rocking through her were everything she would have ever imagined in being with Niko. She knew if ever they had sex, it would be perfect.

Pressure mounted. She welcomed it and felt herself being pushed to the edge of ecstasy. Niko's lips latched on to her column of her neck. There was a firm tugging on her as he sucked. She entwined her fingers in the hair at the base of his neck and angled her head away to give him better access.

She cried out, sensing a wave of heat flood her. There was no more controlling her body. Niko's fingers went deeper, hitting the perfect spot to send her tumbling over into oblivion.

Kizzie's cry echoed through the room. Her muscles grew tight, her orgasm taking hold of her. Niko's fingers continued their assault on her pussy, her release flying from her. Wetness ran down her thighs, but she didn't care.

Niko's hand finally paused. Kizzie leaned her head forward when he lifted his. She rested on his chest, trying to catch her breath. Niko withdrew his hand from between her legs.

"Never would have pegged you for a squirter," Niko said.

Kizzie's eyes flew open. She pushed backed away from him and took in the wetness on his abdomen. Her eyes widened at the amount.

"Oh. My. God," she whispered. There was a lot of it, too. It coated his abdomen and her legs. She bit her lip and tried to hold back a laugh.

Niko's eyes crinkled in the corners as that sexy smile she missed so much appeared. She tried to shove him out of the way so she could get down from the counter.

"I have paper towels over—"

"We don't need them." He stepped back and helped her down but didn't move away from her. His larger body kept her against the counter. He reached up and cupped her chin. "Baby, messy is good."

Even his words had her getting more turned on.

She grew still, lost in his eyes. She was mesmerized by them. How long had she waited for him to look at her the way he was?

Forever.

She inhaled slowly and found herself leaning on

him. He lowered his head and kissed her. This time it was languid and thorough. Niko's tongue stroked hers. She faintly felt his hands draw her panties down past her hips. Kizzie moaned, ghosting her hands along his back and down to his waist. She hooked her fingers underneath the edge of his briefs and pushed them down.

Niko's cock popped free, and it was a sight to behold. It was just as she had thought. Long and thick. Her heart stuttered. She took in the chunky vein that ran along the underside of it. The stiff member aimed toward the ceiling. She reached out. She could barely fit her fingers around it. The skin was hot to touch, and the second she moved her hand to the base of his shaft, Niko's hand shot out and stopped her.

"Not right now," he grunted.

She pouted and gave him a squeeze before he peeled her fingers off him.

He spun her around and forced her hands on the counter. "Those stay here."

"Not fair."

"I'm going to make it all better. I promise," he said.

"But..." Her words ended on a moan.

Niko slid his smooth, warm shaft along the

seam of her ass. She bit her lip from the feeling of him repeating the motion. Her breaths were coming more rapid along with her heart rate increasing.

Niko's hands came around and molded to her breasts. His lips pressed on the side of her neck, and he continued to move behind her. Kizzie released the counter, wanting to touch him somehow.

"I said, hands on the counter," Niko growled.

He snatched her hand off his hip and put it back where it had been. His foot came between hers and pushed her legs wider. He nipped her shoulder with his teeth, pushing her forward. His hand was in the center of her back, holding her in place. She was completely at his mercy and she had no complaints. The broad head of his cock slid along her slick folds.

"Now keep your hands where I put them, and you can have this."

Kizzie whimpered.

She wouldn't dare move.

The fucking house could be burning to the ground around them and she wouldn't budge a muscle.

That was how much she wanted to feel his cock inside her. That thick cock belonged in her pussy.

Niko thrust slightly, sending the full length of him against her labia. She shivered, the ache in her core returning. He may have made her climax on his hand, but now she wanted to explode with his cock in her pussy.

"Are you going to move?"

"No," she whispered.

She held her breath the second she felt him line the mushroom tip to her opening. The air escaped her when he surged forward. She cried out from the slight burn of her walls stretching to accommodate him. He withdrew slightly then sank deeper. When he was fully seated, he held still.

Kizzie closed her eyes, basking in the sensation of Niko. Her pussy had never been stretched so wide before. The pain was still there but was lessening. She celebrated that she was able to take him. She would have to admit for a slight second, she'd thought he might be too big for her.

Where there is a will, there is a way.

"Fuck, you feel so good around me."

He groaned, and she clenched her muscles around him. There was nothing sexier than hearing a man enjoy himself and moan during sex. The hand on her back slid up and entwined itself in her hair, his other hand resting on her hip.

"Do that again."

She performed her kegal maneuver again,

thankful that she did them religiously. Kizzie squeezed him tight, flexing her muscles around him.

Niko withdrew slightly, thrusting forward, eliciting a cry from Kizzie.

"Yes," she hissed.

The hold he had on her hair kept her in place while he repeated his motion. His strokes were deep, fast, and Kizzie was willing to take everything he gave her.

Her cries filled the air; she was unable to contain them. His cock was doing a number on her. Her clit, stimulated from his motion, sent her racing toward another climax. Kizzie gasped, her eyes shut tight, and she allowed Niko to fuck her.

"Kizzie," Niko moaned.

Her heart leaped at the sound of her name spilling from his lips. His pace increased. His grip on her tightened. Kizzie kept her hands where they were supposed to be but used her leverage on the counter to push back on Niko. The move sent him unbelievably deeper.

"Oh," she cried.

Now that she'd done this first move, she couldn't stop. Niko's nails dug into her hip as he continued to pound in her. Kizzie's breast swayed freely with each thrust of his hips. She kept up the pace, meeting him stroke for stroke.

Kizzie couldn't take it any longer. Her muscles grew tight, her mouth opened, and a scream released from her. Intense heat spread through her body, starting at the crown of her head and racing all the way down to her toes. An electric current rippled its way through her body, and she trembled uncontrollably.

Niko cried out her name again. Her head was yanked back by his hold. He roared through his release, sending waves of his thick seed into her. A few pumps later, Niko lodged himself inside her.

Only the sounds of their heavy panting filled the air. Dribbles of fluid slid down her inner thighs. She inhaled and tried to control her breathing. Her muscles were contracting around him. She loved the feeling of him and didn't want him to leave her.

Niko released her hair, and her head tilted forward. He withdrew from her, and instantly, she felt open, as if a missing piece was lost. Niko wrapped an arm around her and turned her toward him. Her knees were weak, and her arms dangled by her sides like loose noodles. She leaned into him, uncertain if she could support her own weight.

"You know I planned this, right?" she whispered. Kizzie still couldn't believe they had finally crossed the line. It had been everything she had imagined. There were so many times she had fantasized about being with Niko. Her imagination didn't compare to the real thing.

Her skin was slick with sweat, her thighs coated in their release, her pussy tingling in ways she didn't know it could, and her heart—it was no longer hers.

She had known for years that she was in love with Niko.

There was no turning back. If he walked away from her this weekend, he'd take her heart with him.

No negative thoughts, she whispered to herself.

Niko would never hurt her. There had always been a connection between them. The night he had stepped in and saved her from that asshole, Kizzie had known they were meant to be a part of each other's lives forever.

"Is that so?" Niko arched an eyebrow at her. His hand moved down to cup her ass, holding her close to him.

"Yeah." She raised her arms and entwined her fingers at the base of his neck. Her breasts were crushed between them. She loved the feeling of his hardened body against hers. "I had this grand scheme to treat you to a good time then seduce you into my bed."

That sexy lopsided grin of his appeared. He gazed around the kitchen before turning his attention back to her.

"This doesn't look like your bedroom."

Kizzie grinned and rubbed herself on him. Niko growled and bent down and hefted her up into his arms. She wrapped her legs around his waist, tightened her arms around his neck, and leaned in by his ear.

"Niko Rusek. Carry me to my room and fuck me again with that big cock of yours."

He barked a laugh and spun on his heels. Kizzie squealed and held on as he marched through her home in the direction of her bedroom.

four

Kizzie held on to Niko while he carried her through her small home. She nestled her face in the crook of his neck and laved her tongue along his neck. She journeyed up to his ear and nipped it with her teeth.

"Hurry," she moaned.

Her breasts were crushed between them with his hands on her ass. He stalked down the hallway. The excitement that filled her went all the way to her core. She needed to have him deep inside her again. One time certainly wouldn't do. Now she had him, she was going to take full advantage of that monster cock.

Kizzie moaned, her body already preparing for him. The remnants of their coupling coated her thighs, but it was the new sensation of her wetness seeping from her core. She slid her fingers up and buried them in his hair.

"Niko," she exhaled.

"Fuck," he muttered.

They arrived at her bedroom door, but instead of crossing the threshold into the room, she found herself pressed against the wall. Niko captured her lips with his in a hard kiss. His tongue swept in and dominated every aspect of the kiss. Her breath was snatched from her as he took everything from her. His cock brushed her slit, and it elicited a cry from her.

Soon, he was driving forth and sinking his cock into her. Their grunts and moans filled the air once he was seated fully. Kizzie tore her lips from his and leaned her head back on the wall. Her breaths were coming in pants. It didn't make any sense how good he felt in her pussy.

That slight burn was back, and this time Kizzie welcomed it with open arms. It was something she could get used to.

Niko's mouth was on her neck, allowing her hands to dive in his hair. She shifted her hips and pushed them forward. Niko withdrew his length from her, only leaving the tip in before he thrust forward, hard.

"Oh!" she cried out.

Kizzie's legs tightened around his waist. Niko's hands tightened on her, digging deep into her flesh and pounding into her. She would have bruising in the morning, but she didn't care. No one would be seeing her naked ass.

"Bed."

She had expected that he would put her down to allow her to walk, but of course, Niko did what he wanted. Somehow, the man stayed buried in her and walked them into her bedroom. With it being summer, it was still bright outside, and they didn't have to turn any lights on. Niko navigated across her room. Each step caused her to moan from the jostling and slight movement of his cock buried deep. It wasn't until he needed to put her down on her bed that he withdrew from her.

"Kizzie. Kizzie. Kizzie," Niko murmured.

She shuffled backward to the middle of the bed. She allowed her legs to fall wide apart, exposing herself. She felt wanton and unrestrained with Niko. She didn't feel embarrassed at what she may look like. The heat in his gaze was all that she needed to feel beautiful.

Her gaze dropped down to that mammoth appendage of his that was standing erect. She licked her lips, unable to turn away from it. He called her name again. His blue eyes were fastened on her. He knelt on the edge of the bed and made his way to her. Kizzie propped herself up on her elbows. He lowered between her thighs, his cock brushing her stomach.

Niko pushed her down and hooked her legs on his forearms, spreading her wide for him. She inhaled sharply at the sensation of his cock nudging at her entrance.

"Did you plan all of this?" he asked.

Niko surged forward, sinking into her. She closed her eyes momentarily, then focused in on him. His cock was lodged completely in her. This new angle allowed her to feel all of him. There was no room separating their pelvic areas.

"Yes," she hissed.

He smirked and withdrew, slamming back into her. Kizzie cried out, and her instincts had her trying to back away. It was way too much. He was going too deep.

She almost laughed at herself. Here she had thought she was big and bad enough to take all of Niko.

"Where do you think you're going?" Niko growled.

She had no control over her legs since he had them propped up on his arms. He guided her legs up and farther apart and thrust again.

She was truly at his mercy and she no longer cared. Niko Rusek could do whatever he wanted to her. If she died today, she would go out as one happy woman. What would they put on her headstone?

Here lies a woman who was split in half by a thick cock.

"How long? Tell me how long you've wanted this," he grunted. His hips jerked faster.

She welcomed the harsh jolts. She reached out and grabbed the blanket underneath her. She needed something to hold on to.

"Years," she admitted.

Tears slid out of her eyes. They weren't tears of pain, but of pure joy, happiness, and ecstasy. She was finally able to be honest with Niko. This might not be the ideal time to admit how long she'd wanted him, how long she'd lusted after him, and how long she'd loved him.

"Kizzie, you should have said something." He pushed her legs out of the way and lowered himself to her. He rested his elbows on the either side of her head. His hips continued shunting while he pressed hard kisses to her lips.

Kizzie wrapped her arms around his neck and cupped his face.

"I wasn't sure you looked at me like a woman," she admitted, her lips brushing his.

He paused his thrusts and stared at her with a confused expression.

"What the fuck is that supposed to mean? How else am I supposed to view you?" he asked.

It was hard to concentrate on the question. Kizzie didn't want him to stop fucking her. She shifted her hips and lifted them off the bed. The move meant his shaft slid against her slick walls.

"More than a friend."

"Friends don't do what we are doing," Niko murmured.

His hips pistoned again. His strokes were long and deep. There was no more talking. Not that they need to. Something passed between them that Kizzie couldn't explain. It was like they both understood they had crossed the point of no return.

Nothing would ever be the same after this.

Kizzie's body shook. She clenched her eyes shut, basking in the sensation rushing through her.

"Kizzie," Niko moaned.

His pace quickened, and a roar tore from his lips. Her eyes flew open the second she felt his muscles grow taut and a warmth flood inside her. His hips continued thrusting as he filled her up with his release. His eyes were clenched tight, his head thrown back.

Niko reaching his release sucked every inch of breath out of her lungs. She couldn't take her eyes off him. It was a beautiful sight to see.

She wasn't even mad he'd come without her. She was actually pleased that it was her making this sexy man reach his climax. What woman wouldn't want bragging rights about her magical pussy?

"Shit, Kizzie. I didn't mean to do that," Niko panted.

He fell forward, catching himself before he landed on her. He rested on his forearms above her. His semisoft cock was still buried deep, his release slowly seeping out of her and running down toward the mattress.

"What are you apologizing for?" She kissed his lips softly.

The man had given her two out-of-this-world orgasms when they were in the kitchen. As far as she was concerned, they were even. In her past relationships, the guys hadn't known her clit from her labia, much less give her an orgasm. Niko, on the other hand, didn't need any instructions on getting her off.

She offered him a smile, seeing the grumpy Niko was returning. "I don't mind. I'm good."

His only response—a grunt.

He withdrew his cock, and she offered a protest. Kizzie held back a grimace at the sensation of more of his release sliding out of her. How much cum did the man make? She was going to need a shower for sure tonight. There was so much of their juices and release on her. Kizzie could feel the stickiness on her inner thigh. At this point, she didn't know what was on her.

He pushed up on the bed to where he knelt between her legs. A questionable glint appeared in his eyes. A smirk appeared on his lips, and she grew worried.

What was he up to?

"Niko, I said it was fine. It happens." She shrugged nonchalantly. She suddenly wished she hadn't said anything.

His eyes darkened and narrowed on her.

He didn't like that.

"You should know me better than anyone,

Kizzie," Niko said. He shifted on the bed to where he was lying on the mattress with his face eye level to her pussy.

Kizzie began to panic. Didn't he see all the stuff on her? She could feel it, so he had to see it.

"I always take care of you."

"What are you doing?" She tried to sit up and close her legs, but Niko wasn't having any of it.

His large hands easing her thighs back open. Kizzie landed back on her elbows. Her eyes flew to the open door of her bedroom. Her bathroom was located across the hall. She could run across in seconds.

"Let me go get a towel."

"Lie down," he snapped.

She fell back from his slight shove. Her mouth opened in shock. His fingers spread her labia apart, exposing her clit. Kizzie's back arched off the bed from the first contact of his tongue. It slithered through her slit and made its way to her clit. He suckled her swollen nub into his mouth. She moaned, basking in the pleasure that spread through her.

"Niko," she chanted. Her eyes rolled into the back of her head. She turned herself over to Niko.

How did she get to be so lucky?

He released her clit and sent his tongue through her slit again. She exhaled a shaky breath. She couldn't think of anything else but Niko and his face buried between her thighs and that tongue of his.

Again, this man needed no coaching or instructions. It was like he knew what made her tick. His lips closed around her clit again, her body jerking. Her legs were still pressed apart with his hands resting on her inner thighs while he feasted on her.

Kizzie's hips moved on their own accord, and she rode his tongue. Her body trembled and shook. Kizzie freed one hand from her blanket and entwined her fingers in Niko's thick dark hair. Her moans filled the air, and she wasn't ashamed of being verbal with her pleasure. There was no better way to reward her lover than to let him hear how well she was enjoying what he was doing to her.

It didn't take long before Kizzie was screaming through her next orgasm. Her body slick with sweat, she fell back onto the mattress. Her eyes were closed while she focused on her breathing. Niko slowly licked her clit and everything that was between her legs. A small smile appeared on her lips.

She hadn't pegged him to be so damn nasty, but hell, she had benefited from it, so she wasn't going to complain.

five

Niko stared down at the sleeping woman in his arms. This was where Kizzie belonged. He had always known it but had tried to ignore it. All the women over the years were just placeholders. He had never intended to commit to any of them. With Kizzie, she meant the world to him, and he hadn't wanted to fuck things up with her. She was the best thing that had ever happened to him.

A soft snore escaped her. She snuggled closer to him as if seeking him out unconsciously. Ever since the first night they had met, he'd always protected her. She was a beautiful woman, and he just couldn't believe she would think he had looked at her as anything but.

Niko brought her flushed to his body. He wanted to meet each of her needs.

Even the ones she exhibited unconsciously.

Kizzie should have known that she was the only woman who he truly cared about. He was the one she called on for everything. Be it listening to her rant and rave over her current boyfriend or dating disaster to a hard day at work and she needed someone to talk to. An outing with her girlfriends and she was too plastered to drive home, it was Niko who'd ensured she'd got home safe.

Anything she'd ever needed, he'd provided.

He had never thought of settling down and starting a family. The only example of a family he'd had was his broken home. He would never submit a woman and children to what his father had done. Maybe that was why he'd never said anything about his feelings to Kizzie.

He had his old man's blood running through his veins.

Kizzie moved again, and he bit back a groan. Her naked body against his had him thinking carnal thoughts. Everything about her was perfect. From her bright smile, spunky personality, to her full breasts, wide hips, and a tight pussy that was made to take his cock.

Their night together had been an experience of a lifetime. Niko would have to admit that he had only ever fucked women before. With Kizzie, there was more to it than sex. There was a deep bond between them. She was the only woman he had ever allowed to get close to him. Besides his brother, there was no other person in the world who knew the real Niko.

She was the one.

Why had it taken him so long to realize it? He had no clue but he was going to rectify it. Kizzie was his, and he was going to make sure she knew it.

Niko's gaze was drawn to her soft lips. They were plump and parted slightly. Her breathing pattern was beginning to change. She would soon be awakening. She had been asleep for a couple of hours. She had gone out like a light immediately after her last orgasm. It had been torture to keep his hands to himself and allow her to rest.

He shouldn't touch her again. She was going to be sore in the morning. He had been too rough with her. Kizzie's pussy had been so tight, it was a wonder he hadn't spilled his seed the first second he'd entered her. His cock grew thick remembering how it had felt to be lodged deep in her.

Kizzie's eyes fluttered open. They were still

heavy with sleep and out of focus. She blinked a few times until her gaze settled on him.

"Have you been watching me the entire time I've been dozing?" Kizzie's voice was sexy with a deep huskiness added to it. She tilted her head back slightly and held his gaze.

"Maybe." Niko didn't need much rest, and watching Kizzie while she slumbered had been rewarding. The last time they had made love, she had climaxed on his cock while riding him and immediately had crashed out sprawled across him. Niko had been buried deep inside her and had to withdraw from her and reposition her.

Kizzie could be a hard sleeper. She hadn't even flinched when he had moved her to lie beside him.

"Creep." She snickered. The teasing glint in her eyes was bright.

Kizzie's infections laugh and personality was one of the things he loved about her. Even when he was in the darkest of moods, Kizzie wouldn't bat an eye. She would have him feeling better in no time.

"Am I?" He arched an eyebrow. He rolled over onto her.

She immediately widened her legs to accommodate him. He settled over her with his arms taking most of his weight. She winced, and he thoughts were confirmed.

"You're sore?"

He brushed her wayward hair away from her face. She nodded slightly. Her teeth snuck out and snagged her bottom lip.

"Yeah, I am," she admitted.

Niko dropped a kiss to her lips before moving to sit on the side of the bed. The bed shifted behind him. He looked over his shoulder and found her resting up on her elbows, staring at him.

"Where are you going?"

He stood and walked out of the room. He went into her bathroom and grabbed one of her hand towels that were hanging along the wall. He took it and tossed it in the sink and ran cold water on it. He waited until it was fully drenched then picked it up and wrung it out.

This would have to do for now.

He returned to the room and found her resting back on the pillows. She had the look of a woman who had been royally fucked. Niko held back a smirk. Pride filled his chest. There was something that must be ingrained in his male DNA that had him wanting to pound on his chest.

"Spread your legs." He sat on the edge of the bed with the rolled towel in his hand.

"That's why I'm sore now," she sassed.

He narrowed his eyes on her. That mouth of hers was going to get her in trouble. His gaze dropped down to her swollen lips, and memories surfaced from last night.

Fuck.

Kizzie sucking his cock had solidified that his heart and soul belonged to her. Niko blinked and came back to the present. He couldn't be thinking of such things when he was trying to help her.

"Kizzie." He leered at her with his best serious expression he could make.

She rolled her eyes and pulled back the covers. She bit her lip and allowed her legs to drop open. It took everything Niko had to keep his cock from swelling, but it was a losing battle. His dick had a mind of its own, and when it came to Kizzie, it did what it wanted.

He placed the towel, ignoring her sharp intake of breath. She closed her legs to keep it in place.

"Is that better?" he asked.

"Yeah, for now," she said. She leaned back on the pillow. Her deep-brown eyes were still filled with sleep. She hadn't gotten that much.

Niko's gaze perused her body, taking in the darkening marks along her neck and breasts. He didn't know why, but the need to mark her had come over him. He reached out and touched the side of her neck gently with his finger. The bruise would soon deepen.

"That dick of yours needs to come with a warning label."

Her giggle filled the air. Niko chuckled at her little joke. He tilted her chin up to meet his eyes.

"Yeah?" Where did she come up with this stuff? No matter what, she could always find the humor in situations. That was why he was in love with her.

He was in love with Kizzie McCall.

No matter how many times he said it in his mind, he was still in awe.

"Don't get it twisted. I'd do it again." She fell back in a fit of laughter.

He could only shake his head at her. What was he going to do with her? She finally stopped laughing and just stared at him. They fell into a comfortable silence.

"Niko, we need to talk."

He nodded in agreement. He slid into the bed next to her and brought her into the crook of his arm. She leaned her head on his chest, a sigh escaping her. He dropped a kiss to the top of her head.

"Come back to San Francisco," he murmured.

Kizzie stiffened in his arms. He knew what he was asking was a bit much, but he was dead serious. She belonged with him.

"What?" Kizzie lifted her head. She studied him for a moment before relaxing again. "You're serious."

He tipped her chin up higher and held her gaze.

"I need you with me. Nothing has been the same since you left. You're all I think about, and I've come to realize that you belong with me," he said truthfully. He wasn't a man of many words, but he believed in honesty. He was going to lay all of his cards on the table tonight.

He was not going back to California without her.

Determination filled Niko. He would do whatever he needed in order to get her to say yes to coming home with him. Her family may be here in Cleveland, but her home was back in San Francisco with him.

"You're all I think about, too, Niko." She took his hand in hers and entwined their fingers together. She brought it up to her lips and kissed the back of his hand. "But I don't think things between us will be the same. We can't go back to the way it was."

"I don't want it the way it was before," he admitted. That was the honest truth. He didn't want her out dating other men and he certainly didn't even want to look at or touch another woman. The only woman he wanted was this one right here. With her soft brown skin, sexy body, and the sweetest pussy he'd ever tasted.

"Well then, how do you want it?" she asked.

"You and me."

The room fell silent. Kizzie stared at him, and he wasn't even sure she was breathing. He combed his fingers through his hair and blew out a deep breath. His chest tightened with worry. All of this was new to him. He had never been in a predicament where he was unsure if a woman wanted to be with him.

"You and me?" Kizzie echoed. Her big brown eyes were as round as saucers. Tears teetered on the edges of her eyelids. "What are you saying, Niko?" she whispered.

There was no time better than the present. If he was going to convince her to come back home with him, then he would tell her what he should have told her before she left.

"I'm in love with you, Kizzie. I need you in my

life, not only as my best friend but as my woman." He cupped her face gently and brushed aside the lone tear that traveled down her cheek. He hated seeing her tears, and the fact that he was the one causing her to cry had him panicking. "Why are you crying? Tell me what's wrong and I'll fix it."

"There's nothing that needs fixing." She sniffed. Her hand came up to rest on his. Her lips curved up into a soft smile. She leaned her face into his palm. "Everything is just right."

"Then why the tears?" He wiped another one from her cheek. He didn't know what else to do at the moment. There was no one for him to go after for making her cry. If everything was fine as she'd said, then why was she crying? "I don't understand."

"Niko. These are not tears of pain or sorrow. They are tears of joy. The man I love just told me that he loves me."

He paused and stared into her eyes. His mouth grew dry. Did he just hear what he thought he'd heard? She loved him? Her smile widened into a grin.

"Tell me again," he said. This woman, who was damn near perfect, loved him? How had he ever gotten so lucky in life?

"Niko Rusek, I love you," she whispered.

Niko gathered Kizzie to him and covered her lips with his. Her lips parted and welcomed his tongue. He poured all of his feelings into this kiss. There was no better feeling than knowing Kizzie was in love with him, but there was one thing he had to know.

"Will you come home with me?" he asked.

"I'll talk to my father, but I'm sure he will be okay with losing me as an employee." She chuckled.

He swooped in again and kissed her. He pulled her onto his lap to sit sideways. She took the towel from between her legs and tossed it onto the floor.

"This will be hell moving back to Cali, but you, Mr. Rusek, are worth it."

"You're damn right I am."

She could leave everything here for all he cared. He could buy her whatever she wanted and needed once they were back home. Everything was going to be perfect. He'd have his woman with him, and there was nothing else he needed in life.

"But what am I going to do for a living? I doubt I'll be able to get my old job back," she said. She entwined her arms around his neck.

Niko, frankly, hadn't cared for her old job. She had been stressed, overworked, and underpaid.

Going back there was not an option as far as he was concerned.

"Why do you need to search for a job? You can come work at the shop," he said.

He and Will had been re-evaluating their needs for the shop and were due to start hiring more help. Business was booming, and with their reputation, they were only going to grow as time moved on. With her business background, she would be an asset to their company.

"You have gotten it all figured out, don't you?" she asked.

She reached up and combed her fingers through his hair. A shiver rippled down his spine at her touch. He wrapped his arm around her waist to keep her balanced. The softness of her ass had his cock growing stiff. He tried to ignore it. As long as she remained still, he would be fine. Otherwise, it would have to be a cold shower for him until she wasn't sore.

"Of course I do. Don't I always take care of you?" He smirked.

"And I'm going to assume you want me moving into your house?" She arched her perfectly sculpted eyebrows.

"Why do you think I did all the repairs and updates you suggested?"

Kizzie's mouth dropped open, but no words came out.

What he'd said was true.

He had been planning this since the moment she'd left. Kizzie had loved the home he had purchased. She had spent much time there and had even claimed a spare room as hers for the nights she didn't want to go home. That home was too large for just him. He had never minded when she'd stayed, and when she had, she'd usually cooked for them.

That home was meant for a family.

It was never meant to be for a single guy. That home needed love and the pitter-patter sounds of children's feet running through it. His gut clenched at the thought of Kizzie growing round with his child. For all he knew they could have already created a baby. He hadn't used protection. It hadn't even crossed his mind. He had never had sex without a rubber. Will had taught him to never go out and play in the rain without a raincoat.

But with Kizzie, he was willing to take the chance. His gaze dropped down to her stomach, and he honestly hoped they had created a little one.

Kizzie would make a wonderful mother. He wasn't getting any younger, and a few kids with Kizzie sounded damn good.

He and his brother were lucky. They had made it out of a life of abuse and had grown up to make something out of themselves. Not many could do what they had. They were successful and had everything they needed.

Now he had Kizzie.

His life was complete.

"Cat got your tongue?" He reached up and tipped her chin up to close her mouth.

"You are sneaky. You know how much I love your home." Her small hand shoved his shoulder gently.

He grabbed her hand and kissed her palm. "It's our home."

"You know just what to say, don't you," she teased. Kizzie kissed his lips. There were no more tears. Just happiness and excitement filled her eyes. "I'm sure when I get back there are going to be some things I will want to change."

"Take my credit card and do what you want."

She squealed and wiggled around on his lap, doing a little dance. She cupped his face and pressed a hard kiss to his lips.

"Tell me again!"

"You can take my credit card?" He held back a laugh when her smile disappeared.

She shoved him again with a scowl forming.

"You know what I mean." She rolled her eyes and pouted slightly.

Niko brought her close to him where his lips brushed hers. "Kizzie McCall, I love you."

"I'll never get enough of hearing you say that," she whispered. Kizzie rested her forehead on his.

"And I'll never tire of saying it."

epilogue

Kizzie glanced down at the sparkling diamond wedding set that rested on her ring finger. Niko had proposed to her two months after she had moved back to San Francisco. It had been a total surprise. They had taken a ride out on his bike that night after dinner and they had driven down to Pier 7 where they had parked and gone for a walk. It was there he had gotten down on one knee and asked her to marry him.

She of course had said yes.

They were married two months after that. Neither of them had wanted an elaborate wedding. They had an intimate ceremony with their closest friends and family on Baker Beach.

She sat back in her office at Precision Motors.

True to his word, Niko and Will had hired her to be the shop's business manager. Her little office wasn't much. There was no window view of downtown San Francisco like she used to have at her former job. She didn't need it. She had painted and made it as homey as she could. The shop was full of men, grease, and motorcycles. Her office fit her personality with bright colors and simple modern furniture.

Everything in her life was perfect.

Kizzie sat back and rested her hand on her round belly. A giggle spilled from her lips. By her calculations, she had returned from Cleveland with more than a new husband.

They had created a little bundle of joy.

Their son was due to make his appearance in just over a month. Kizzie was impatient and couldn't wait to meet her tiny man. Niko was the anxious first-time father. Their boy wasn't even here yet, and he'd already baby-proofed the house, upped security around their home, and read every parenting book he could get his hands on.

Kizzie was confident he was going to make a great father.

Glancing down at her desk, she took in the numbers she had just run. She needed to review them with him before she signed off on the latest purchases for the shop. She would show Will, but he was out with a realtor, searching for a new building for the second shop they were going to be opening.

Pushing back from her desk, she walked over to her door and opened it. She waddled her way through it and went on the hunt for her husband. She could have been lazy and used the overhead speaker, but she needed to get up and walk. Sitting in a chair all day wasn't good for her back.

"Hey, Kizzie!" Solomon, one of the young apprentices, waved to her. He was mopping the floor around one of the empty workstations. It was very important to Will and Niko to take in young kids and help them find a trade.

"Morning, Solomon." She waved at him and paused near him.

He was a good kid and would make a great mechanic one day. He was being raised by a single mother who had two jobs. Precision Motors kept this kid off the street on the weekends and after school. Solomon practically lived here and thrived here.

"Have you seen my husband?"

"Last I saw, he was working on bay seven."

"Thank you!" She spun on her heel headed

toward the back of the shop. The baby chose that moment to give her a real good kick. She grimaced and rubbed the area with her hand. She arrived at bay seven where a large monster of a bike sat. Her breath caught in her throat at the sight of Niko standing next to it. His great Precision Motors t-shirt molded to his perfectly sculpted chest and put his tattooed arms on full display. Her gaze slid down and took in his jeans and boots.

He glanced up and combed a hand through his dark hair. It was slightly longer than he usually kept it. She had no complaints with it.

Her man was downright sexy.

Her core clenched, and she immediately grew aroused.

"What's wrong?" Niko frowned. His gaze homed in on her hand resting on her stomach.

She removed it immediately and gave a short laugh.

"Nothing. The baby just kicked really hard," she said.

She felt breathless as she made her way over to him. This sexy man was hers forever. She smiled and stopped next to him. He reached out and cupped her swollen belly. His strong hands gently rubbed it. She inhaled sharply at his touch.

She had read that many women didn't want their partners touching them this late in their pregnancy. Kizzie was the complete opposite. She was hornier than ever. She craved Niko's touch.

"Are you working too hard?" he asked.

"What?" She choked back a laugh. Her husband was extremely protective of her. He wouldn't hesitate in sending her home if he thought she was overdoing it. She rose on her tiptoes and kissed his chin. "I'm fine. I was coming to find you. I need your approval on the order I'm about to place."

"I'm sure it will be fine. Just order whatever you think we need." He cupped her cheeks and dropped a kiss on her forehead.

She leaned into him, resting her hands on his waist. She was appreciative that he had put his full trust in her, but she was still a relatively new employee and needed to double-check things.

"Niko," she whispered.

A few of the other mechanics were nearby, working. Her belly pressed into his as she tried to get closer to him. His gaze narrowed on her, and she was sure he was picking up on her vibe.

"You said when I need you, to come find you so you can help me."

She winked at him. The corner of his lip went up

slightly. He got her point. He looked around before taking her by the hand.

"So you need me to review the order?" he asked nonchalantly.

They ambled through the shop as if it were any other day. Inside, Kizzie was burning up. She wanted to drag her man behind her and toss him in her office.

But she couldn't exactly do that. One, he was too large for her to drag anywhere, and two, her current pregnancy status would keep her from even trying.

"This won't take me long." She smiled.

They had perfected the art of a quickie. Niko's name was continuously called while they made their way through the shop. He had to stop a few times and talk with a few of the employees. Kizzie tried to not let her frustration show. Didn't they see that she needed her man?

Niko returned to her side, and she took his hand in hers and sped up. They finally made it to the bank of offices.

"If one more person calls your name," she muttered.

His chuckle echoed behind her. They entered her office where she promptly shut the door and flicked the lock. She spun around but was met with a hard body pressing into her. Niko lowered his head and captured her lips with his. She bit back a moan at the sensations coursing through her. He dominated the kiss with his tongue stroking hers. Kizzie made short work of pulling his shirt over his head and unbuttoning his jeans.

She threw his shirt onto her desk. "Couch."

She was thankful that she had a small two-seater sofa installed in her office. Early in her pregnancy, she had needed it for short naps when she was experiencing fatigue.

"This pregnancy is making you so damn bossy," Niko murmured. He walked backward toward the sofa with her stalking toward him.

"And you love it," she joked. She couldn't help it. Her body had a mind of its own. She didn't know if it was the hormones, but something made her want sex all the time.

Niko reached the couch, and she gave him a slight push. He fell back with a laugh and spread his legs.

"Come here," he said.

She shook her head and moved to stand between his legs. She snagged a throw pillow from beside him and put it on the floor so she could kneel before him.

"I have other plans right now," she said. Even with her big belly she was determined to get on the floor before him.

Niko didn't argue. He must have seen the determination in her eyes. He helped her down onto the pillow. They worked together to pull his jeans down. His cock broke free, and Kizzie could have wept.

She loved the taste of him. She wasted no time wrapping her hand around him and licking him from the base of his shaft to the tip.

"Fuck, Kizzie," he groaned.

His head fell back against the cushions. She loved seeing him like this, and she took her time sucking him off. She closed her eyes and concentrated on what she was doing. She used both hands to slide along his length while she bobbed her head up and down, taking as much of him into her mouth as she could.

Her core clenched while her wetness slowly trailed out of her. She increased the pace of her hands and mouth. The saltiness of him exploded on her tongue. She moaned, taking him farther into her mouth. Her small hands were soon coated with her saliva. She sucked harder, increasing her pressure on him. A curse escaped Niko's lips, and he pulled his cock from her.

"Come here, now," he growled.

His blue eyes darkened, and his gaze latched on to her. He held out his hand and helped her stand from the floor. It took a few attempts, but they finally got her up. He snagged the bottom of her dress and pulled it over her head.

He paused and stared at her. "Where the hell are your panties?"

"What's the point?" She shrugged.

There was no way she would have gotten away with no bra. Her boobs had grown significantly recently. She grinned at him, watching him shake his head. He lowered her onto his lap. He lifted her and guided the broad head of his cock to her opening. She slowly slid down on him until she was completely seated on him. Kizzie paused and tried to catch her breath.

"Are you sure this won't hurt the baby?" Niko asked. His strong hands gripped her ass.

She rested hers on the back of the couch to have something to hold on to.

"I'm sure," she breathed.

He felt so good inside her. She rotated her hips, eliciting a sharp intake of breath from Niko. He raised her and then brought her down on his cock. She cried out in ecstasy, unable to control herself.

"How the hell are you so damn wet?" he muttered.

Sweat beaded on his forehead as he kept himself restrained. He repeated his action with lifting her up and bringing her down on him. They set a steady rhythm, their breaths quickening.

"I love you," she panted. Her hands dug into the couch, heat flooding her. She wasn't going to last much longer. She rode him harder, needing more. His cock stretched her and fulfilled her all at the same time. Her eyes fluttered closed, and she waited for the words she needed to hear.

"I love you more."

Kizzie had never thought she would be this happy in life. Here she was, with the man she had loved for years. He was her protector, her lover, and her best friend. She couldn't ask for anything more in a man.

Ready for the next book in the Lunchtime Chronicles series? Hot Cakes by S. London is next! Grab Hot Cakes HERE today!

99

a note from the author

Dear reader,

Thank you for reading Polish Boy! I hope you enjoyed Kizzie and Niko's story. How could they resist each other? I had so much fun writing this steamy friends to lovers romance. If you loved their story, do me a favor and pass the word on to your book loving friends. Then do me one more favor and leave a review!

Make sure you continue on with the Lunchtime Chronicles series. If you haven't read any other books, check them out! You won't regret it!

Happy holidays,
Peyton Banks

P.S. Stay tuned! Kizzie's cousin, Mykeisha will be getting her own story in Thick & Beefy!

hot cakes

I'm not a bad boy. I'm a dangerous man.

The Doctor

She saved my life, big mistake.

Now she's my obsession. I want to possess her, own her, but to keep her is to curse her to my fate.

She believes we have a future, but it's a fantasy. I have to protect her from the ones who hunt me.

They're relentless, so I must be ruthless to free her of me.

Jada Reign

He's secretive, intense—guarded. He thinks I'm his savior, but I'm no saint. The way he watches me with those piercing gray eyes, says he wants to be mine. I won't allow him to ignore us. It's crazy, but I'm not above shaking my hot cakes to turn him on and turn him out.

***HOT CAKES* is the next book up in the *Lunchtime Chronicles series!*

Grab Hot Cakes today!

LUNCHTIME CHRONICLES, EP. 58

Perfectly made to order.

Mykeisha McCall has decided that she will just be single. After countless dating disasters and terrible relationships, she had called it quits. It may be time to start adopting cats to keep her company. Before she started going to shelters, she had to make a trip to her alma mater for alumni weekend.

It had been a while since she'd seen some of her college friends, and it was just the getaway she needed.

But she hadn't counted on seeing him.

Nash Fitzpatrick.

The one she'd had a crush on but never said a word.

Nash Fitzpatrick had never forgotten the beautiful Mykeisha. She had been the cool chick to hang out with, and they had been friends. After he had graduated college, they had fallen out of touch. He'd figured she would have been married with children by now, but to his surprise, she was single.

With a weekend to catch up, the two were inseparable, and it was almost like old times. Only this time, they did things friends normally didn't do.

Grab your copy of Thick & Beefy today!

about the author

USA TODAY bestselling author, Peyton Banks, is the alter ego of a city girl who is a romantic at heart. Her mornings consist of coffee and daydreaming up the next steamy romance book ideas. She loves spinning romantic tales of hot alpha males and the women they love. Make sure you check her out!

Sign up for Peyton's Newsletter to find out the latest releases, giveaways and news! Visit www.peyton banks.com/newsletter to sign up!

Want to know the latest about Peyton Banks? Follow her online:

also by peyton banks

Current Free Short Story

Summer Escape

Book Boyfriend Dating Agency

Surgeon Book Boyfriend

Silver Creek Ranch (Shared World)

Wrangling Her Cowboy

Lunchtime Chronicles (Peyton's)

Polish Boy

Thick & Beefy

Rich & Decadent

The Keith Brothers

Mr. Hotness

Mr. Arrogant

Blazing Eagle Ranch Series

Back in the Saddle

Knockin' the Boots

Roping a Cowboy

Country at Heart

Cowboy, Take Me Away

Hard to Forget

<u>Special Weapons & Tactics Series</u>

Dirty Tactics (Special Weapons & Tactics 1)

Dirty Ballistics (Special Weapons & Tactics 2)

Dirty Operations (Special Weapons & Tactics 3)

Dirty Alliance (Special Weapons & Tactics 4)

Dirty Justice (Special Weapons & Tactics 5)

Dirty Trust (Special Weapons & Tactics 6)

Dirty Secrets (Special Weapons & Tactics 7)

Dirty Ultimatum (Special Weapons & Tactics 8)

<u>SWAT boxset, books 1-3</u>

<u>Trust & Honor Series (BWWM)</u>

Dallas

Dalton

<u>A Langdale Christmas</u>

The Christmas Secret

The Christmas Wish

The Christmas Gift

<u>Interracial Romances (BWWM)</u>

Pieces of Me

Hard Love

Retain Me

Silent Deception

<u>African American Romance</u>

Breaking The Rules

<u>Mafia Romance</u>

Unexpected Allies (The Tokhan Bratva 1)

www.ingramcontent.com/pod-product-compliance
Lightning Source LLC
Chambersburg PA
CBHW021720190726
48289CB00008B/2610